Flyin Lion and Friends

The Big Catch

By: David Arnold

Ascent Media Group

One summer morning as I awoke
Before the dawn and rushed to
Put my blue jeans on, I hummed
A tune inside my head.
It was my favorite 'Happy Song'

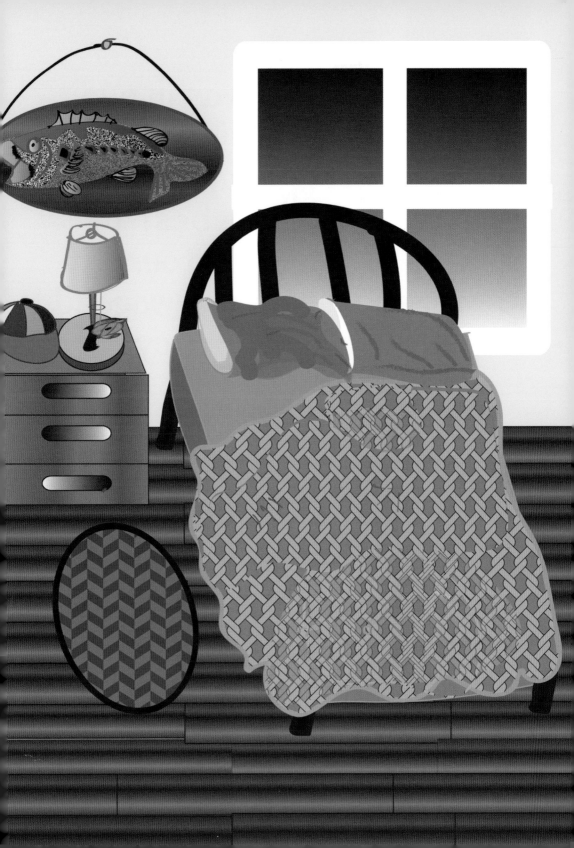

A fishing trip was in our plan so we hurried out at the break of day each of us trying our best to keep up with our four legged friend who wagged his tail along the way.

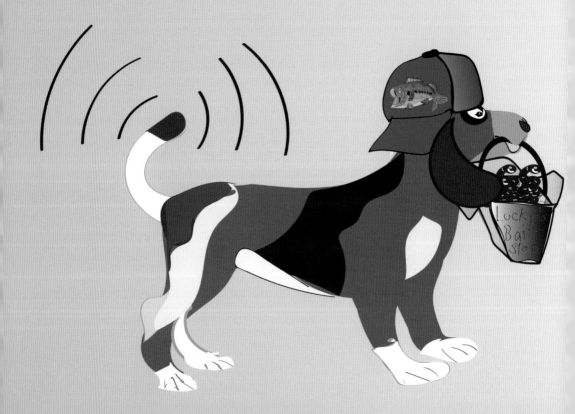

Our favorite spot was not far away so with our hats on our heads and fishing poles in hand we hurried down a familiar path hoping this would be a lucky day!

Each of us keeping rhythm
With the tune we hummed
As down the lane we moved
Along.

Time seemed to crawl yet
We barely noticed and as
For me I kept a secret wish,
That today I'd catch a
Great Big Fish!

Soon I was sitting in a perfect
Spot along the water's bank with
My sister beside me on a bucket
And as we fished we hoped that
With some luck it wouldn't take
Too long before we caught a
Fish or two to take back home.

We watched our corks as
they bobbed up and down
and back and forth and up
and down again and looking
over at our father's face
we saw he had our same
big grin, each of us now
hoping that the fun would
soon begin!

This time we shared
was often quiet and
when dad spoke his
words seemed to float
out into the air sort of
like the lines we cast,
their purpose always
full of care.

It was grand, our fishing hole and a cool morning's breeze when suddenly a real

BIG FISH

leaped from the water right in front of me!

While I know I'm not
supposed to tell a lie
or maybe make a story
up, to me that fish was
bigger than the sky and
I remember very well how
each and every of its
scales from its head unto
its tail sparkled in the
morning's light.

Then to my complete surprise
This great big fish looked at
me right in the eye and gave
What seemed to be a wink.

And faster than you can say
'I'd like a slice of apple pie'
With a flick of its tail it
Broke my line!

As I watched it sink back into the water I realized we were alone again with just our words; me, my sister and our father.

He often used these moments
to help us grow in ways not soon
forgot, by teaching us important
things like being kind to others
and how to tie a fishing knot.

Later while sharing my tall tale of the big catch that got away it seems the best part told was not the fish at all, but the time we spent with dad which was the biggest catch of all.

To this day the memory I can see as clearly as the wink of that big fish's eye is of that old hat that was always on my dad's head or right beside him in his yellow truck where it sat upside down so as not to spill out all his good luck!

That fishing hat that seemed to touch the big blue sky when worn by our dad who taught us to never tell a lie.

For Will and Zoey who have
Their mother's fishing luck!

Ascent Media Group, Inc
3311 Gulf Breeze Parkway #342
Gulf Breeze, FL 32563
Learn More at www.ascentmg.com
ISBN 978-0-9992986-4-0

Written & Illustrated by: David Arnold